THE WITCH BOY

WS

MOLLY KI

Wi
B

OSTERTAG
HE
ECH
OY
graphix
AN IMPRINT OF
SCHOLASTIC

Grandmother
Kieran
Jessamine
Holly
Tohor
Hazel
Linden
Brome
Persimmon
Juniper
Aster

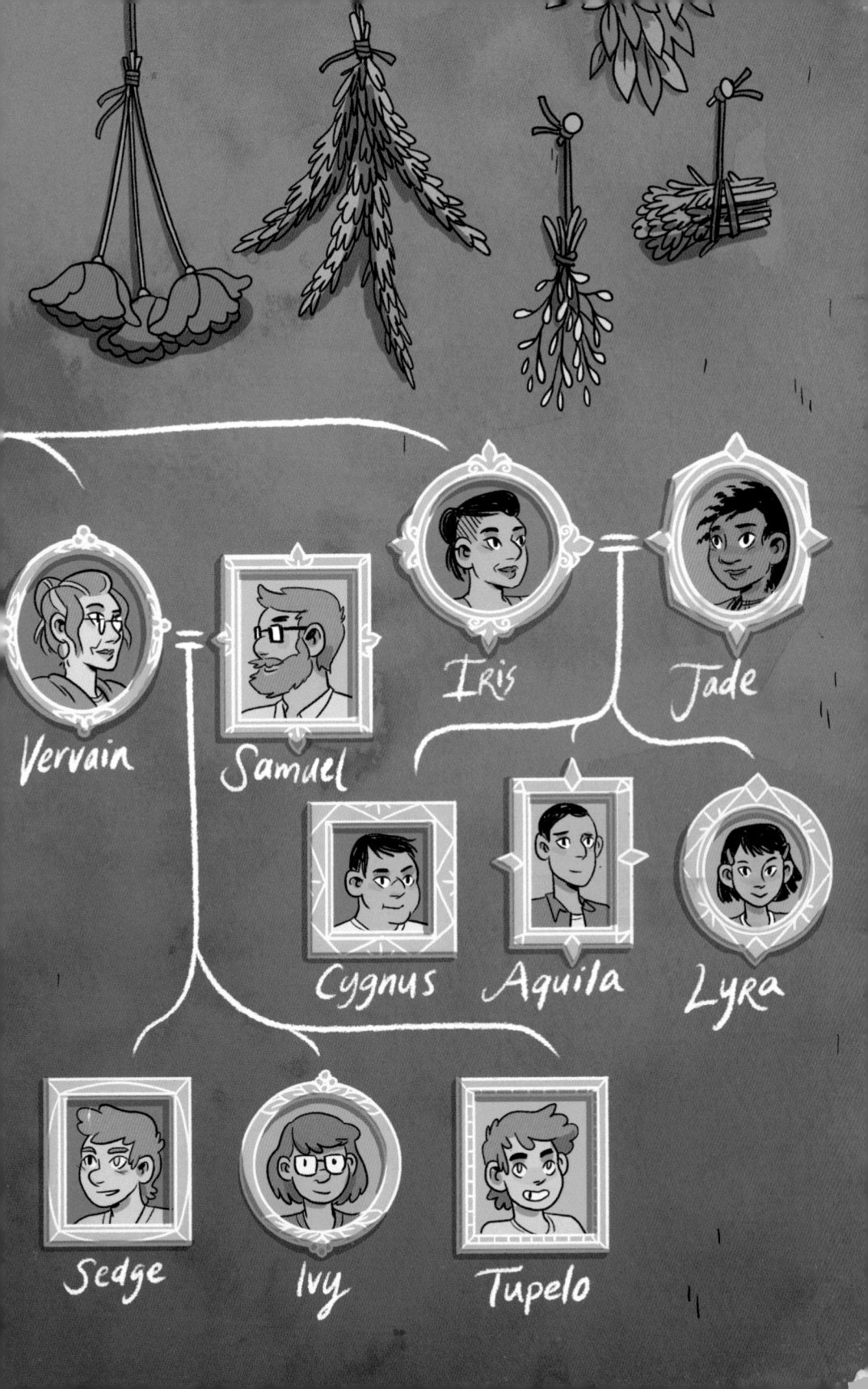
Vervain
Samuel
Iris
Jade
Cygnus
Aquila
Lyra
Sedge
Ivy
Tupelo

This book is dedicated to Wayfinder, the summer camp in upstate New York where I first learned about magic.

Copyright © 2017 by Molly Knox Ostertag

All rights reserved. Published by Graphix, an imprint of Scholastic Inc., *Publishers since 1920*. SCHOLASTIC, GRAPHIX, and associated logos are trademarks and/or registered trademarks of Scholastic Inc.

The publisher does not have any control over and does not assume any responsibility for author or third-party websites or their content.

No part of this publication may be reproduced, stored in a retrieval system, or transmitted in any form or by any means, electronic, mechanical, photocopying, recording, or otherwise, without written permission of the publisher. For information regarding permission, write to Scholastic Inc., Attention: Permissions Department, 557 Broadway, New York, NY 10012.

This book is a work of fiction. Names, characters, places, and incidents are either the product of the author's imagination or are used fictitiously, and any resemblance to actual persons, living or dead, business establishments, events, or locales is entirely coincidental.

Library of Congress Control Number Available

ISBN 978-1-338-08952-3 (hardcover)
ISBN 978-1-338-08951-6 (paperback)

10 9 8 7 6 5 4 18 19 20 21 22

Printed in China 38
First edition, November 2017
Edited by Amanda Maciel
Lettering and color by Molly Knox Ostertag
Additional color by Niki Smith, Barbara Geoghegan, and Shannon Murphy
Book design by Molly Knox Ostertag and Phil Falco
Creative Director: David Saylor

Time for the first lesson of the day, my daughters.

Now, if you are hungry in the forest, you need not despair.
You can convince most trees to blossom and grow fruit, as long as you ask politely and address them using the proper terms.

Who knows the name Apple prefers?
?
Good, Juniper.
Blackberry?
Pear?
Grape?
?
!
?

Once you know the tree's preferred name, you can speak an incantation to request its fruit.
ha ha!
plunk
plunk
And so, you see . . .

Aster!
SWING
HA HA HA HA HA
This lesson isn't for you -- these girls are learning secrets!

But I want to --
Off with you!
HA
HA
HA
HA
HA
HA
HA
Aster, child, what's wrong?

Aunt Vervain caught me again.
I don't understand why Juniper and Hazel and them can all learn how to talk to trees and make potions and do spells and I can't.
It's not *fair*.

But, Aster, that magic isn't *for* you.
How many times do I have to explain that?
But I want to learn it!
Women and men have different types of magic, and witches pass down their knowledge from mother to daughter. That's how it is and how it's always been, my son.
But it's not like there's nothing for you! Soon your shapeshifting will begin, and with it, the ability to see demons and to fight them.
You'll be one of the men.
. . . Don't *want* to shapeshift . . .

sigh
Did you know that Grandmother is a twin?
She had a twin brother.
Mikasi.
Now, Grandmother is very steady and wise, and always has been, but her brother had no patience or wisdom.
He wanted what he couldn't have: his sister's magic.

He spied on her and neglected his lessons.
Although she tried to keep the secrets, he managed to steal spells from her and cast them.
Aster, the spells poisoned his magic, and he lost control.
People were hurt, the house was damaged, and from then on, he could shapeshift, but only into great ferocious beasts which he could not tame.

He was cast out, for he was a danger to himself and the family.
He stole a great treasure before he left and was never seen again.
That's not a story we tell very often.
But . . . I think you need to know it, my son.
I'll not see you turn out like Mikasi.

ha ha
hey!
Aster, we're playing capture the flag and we need one more! You wanna?
Go on, Aster.
pat pat

Why'd Sedge have to go and get Aster? He's never good in this . . .
Okay, so this time let's split up and come at the hill from two angles.
Aquila will probably be their lookout, and he can already shift, so we've got to watch out because he'll probably be a bird --
Why are you in charge, Sedge? Why not let someone who can shift handle the strategy?
Because I'm so charming, obviously!
And I like doing strategies.

Was it part of your brilliant plan to get Aster on our team?
Hey!
Well, it's not like you like this game. You said so yourself last time.
I just think it's stupid that the girls are learning lessons and we're running around in the woods.
Gentlemen, gentlemen!
Linden, you will abide by my decisions as your wise leader, and you can do the strategy next round.
Aster, as you very well know, this is --
What did my Dad say? --
"valuable experience that can be applied to our futures as demon fighters."
Okay, now, Aster, we'll have you on lookout by the henhouse in case they try to get to our flag that way . . .

PULL
apple
pear

Aren't you supposed to tell me not to be doing this?
If you're going to be playing with witchery, at least get it right.
Which one are you, again?
Aster, Grandmother.
Well, just be careful, m'boy.

Hey!
hee hee hee

. . . asked me to make a flower grow in class yesterday, but instead I made the desk start sprouting leaves, so embarrassing . . .
ha
ha ha
I think my dad had to chop that up for firewood! He didn't look happy.

How'd you mess up the spell, Juniper?
Aster . . .
Don't you want to go eat dinner with the other boys?
Hey, guys, isn't that your dad's car?

Aster, go say hi, I'll be there in a sec.
Yeah, okay, I'm going.
Dad!

ha ha
SWING
Oof! You must've grown a foot since I was here last, kid!
CRAK
It wasn't *that* long ago.
Tohor!
Good to see you.
Bleaugh!

You're back so soon!
How are the Nakamoras?
Did the problem end up being a demon after all?
We can talk about work later. I want to know everything that's been going on at home!
Kitchen first. It was a thirsty drive.
I'll be right back --
I was in the middle of a casting; let me just finish it up.

I came back for you, son.
I wanted to help you get ready.
Dad . . . can't you tell me about the demon instead?
Later. I missed you!
Have you been having the dreams yet?
Everyone has dreams.

Animal dreams, Aster.
Animal spirits will come to you in dreams to see if you're fit to receive their gifts.
I had a dream about some bees a few weeks ago.
But I'd just been working in the beehives, so . . .
You came back to help Aster prepare for the Finding?
That's right.
This time you'll Find your first form -- I can smell it!
You Found your form the first time you tried.
Well . . . yes, but plenty of shifters I know tried three, even four years, before a spirit approached them.

Don't worry about it, Aster.
It'll come naturally; there's no sense in fretting.
I'm gonna go. Can we . . . get ready later, Dad?
Of course.

I don't know how to help him.
It's still happening, then?
Sneaking into the girls' lessons and all?
NOD
Give him time. When he's ready, the spirits will Find him and teach him how to shift.
And then he won't have this silly fascination with witchery.
Any son of yours will grow into a good man;
I know that for sure.
smek

splash
splash
splash
pat
pat

It worked!
I mean --
thank you, thank you!
That's a neat trick.

I wasn't doing anything!
Can I have some?
I'm Charlotte. Charlie.
Can you, um . . . not tell anyone you saw that? With the berries?
What did you even do?

You don't go to Sterling Junior High, do you? I'd have recognized you.
No, I, uh . . .
No, I go to a . . . different . . . school.
Um, what happened to your leg?
. . .
You're weird.
I know.
It's okay.
Not, like, creepy-weird.
Just . . . you'd definitely stick out in my school.

You talked to a bush and made it grow blackberries, and that's . . .
well, weird!
But I promise I won't tell anyone.
Not my dads, or anyone at my school, or anyone at your definitely-not-made-up school.
Thanks.
Well, I've gotta go. Bye, berry boy.

Aster! My name is Aster!

For as long as anyone can remember, and longer still, the animal spirits that we share our world with have offered the men of our family a great gift.

We may speak with them, enlist their help, and, most powerful of all, take their gifts and assume their forms.
You will have had dreams where you met with animals and spoke with them.
These were spirits seeking you out, deciding if you were worthy of their favor.

Tonight, on the equinox, you will go out into the forest and seek a spirit of your own.
It may test you; pose you riddles or wrestle for dominance.
If you impress it, it will give you its form to wear.
Stay alert, be clever, and take what is offered.
I know this is your night, my son.

Only beneficial spirits may cross the boundaries of our property.
Tonight, especially, there are demons waiting outside the borders.
Be safe, sons.

peep peep
rustle
peep peep
peep peep
Please.

Please come.
This time, this year, finally, please let me see you.
crunch
crunch

Come on, don't run away from me --
?
Splash

Easy, there, easy.
My name is --
Sedge!
Ssh! I'm talking to an animal spirit.
But the boundaries --

Sedge?
Sedge?

There's neither sign nor scent of him. He must have been taken.
This is a bad night for demons.
I always think it's foolish, having the Finding on this night.

I have to reinforce the boundaries.
You must be pretty shaken up.
I'm okay.
I have to leave tonight.
Warn the Tarwells and the Wildwood clan that something's on the prowl.

Son, before Sedge was taken --
I know what you're going to ask and no, I didn't see any spirits.
I waited and waited but it was just cold and dark and there wasn't anything!

Hey, Juniper.
I'm so sorry you had to see that, Aster . . .
Don't treat me like a baby, you're only three years older.

Three years and two months.
Pat pat
Are you helping Mom?
We're trying to scry for Sedge, me and some of the younger girls.
Scry?
Use magic to look for him.
But none of the normal bowls we use are working, so I'm looking for something else . . .
You look in a bowl?
In water. In a silver bowl, usually. Silver for the moon.
And you reflect the moon in it, and you stir it counter-clockwise, and --

And?
Aha!
And say the person's name.
But you're not supposed to know about that.
You should go to bed, Aster.

SHRUG
SHRUG

HOP

Sedge. Show me Sedge.

This is private. We're here so witches can't spy on us.
??

It's terrible what happened to Sedge, and everyone is working to find him.
But do you know *why* it happened?

He stepped outside the barrier.
That's correct, Tupelo.
We are protected here, because this is a place to be safe and learn.
But outside the standing stones, demons and broken spirits and the fallen roam, preying on humans -- although most people don't know their true nature.
You can't live in this house forever. You must remember that, though they are rare, there are creatures that want to kill you and worse.
That's why it's important to learn to *fight*, and that's why we speak to animal spirits.

You must be strong, because your job will be to protect the humans and the witches from these monsters.
Can't the witches protect themselves?
Sure, with the standing stones and other magics. But witchery takes time, and is better used for other things.
When it comes to battle, to the struggle of life or death . . . that's where we come in.
So tell me . . . did some of you meet animal spirits last night?
Yes, Aquila?

An old badger came to me, and he wanted to wrestle, so I --
-- was a bird, definitely something with feathers, and it told me --
-- so once I caught it, he told me secrets of the treetops and said I would learn his form!

splish
splash

BMP
BMP

BUMP
BUMP

Hey, berry boy!

Can you get my ball?
BMP
Hi, Charlie.

BMP
BANG
Tch!
My name is Aster.
I know.

I was sort of looking for you.
Oh, yeah?
BANG
Come on!
Are you supposed to play that sitting down?
Uh, no, genius. Why don't you try?

TMP
whoosh
Wow, never mind!
Why were you looking for me?
I just . . .
I can't talk to anyone in my house!
I want to . . . help and stuff . . . but everyone thinks I'm a freak.
I'm good at . . . this one thing, but it's a thing that only girls do.
But I'm not *good* at boy stuff, and I just . . .
want to help.

Ugh, tell me about it.
This year at school they stop having co-ed teams, and the guys have way more sports than the girls.
They split stuff up for boys and girls at your school?
Not everything. But sports, yeah, and that's what I really like.
At least I have softball, but . . .
I probably won't get to play this year anyway.
BMP

My family is like that, too. I don't get it.
If you're good at something --
WHOOSH
You should just be allowed to do it!

Can you keep a secret?
Cross my heart and may maggots eat my eyes.
Uh . . . yeah.
Do you have, like, a bowl?
Silver?
?

There is a moon, so maybe this'll work.
I overheard Mom saying it's more about intent than specifics . . .
Okay, I'll try to show you my mom. I think you'd like her.
Mom. Holly.

Whoa. Is that a . . .
How're you doing that?
And that's your house?
It's so funky!
Hey!
Is that . . . magic?
nod
And you're not supposed to do it?
It's a girl thing.
But . . . I really like it. It's not like I can just . . . not do it.

What else can you do?
I don't know a lot of spells. They're secret.
But I can . . .
Well, you saw, I can make fruit grow.
I can scry, and I can light candles, but it doesn't always work.
I can make a little circle of silence -- I use that one a lot to read.
And I can fix broken things.
Like bones?

No, I meant like . . .
broken bowls and things . . .
Could I --
could I pay you or give you something or --
If you could heal my leg . . .
Aster, the doctor said it was a really bad break, and it'll take forever to heal and it still might not be quite right --
Have you seen Aster?

Something's wrong.
Not him, too!
My dads get worried when I stay out late, too. It's probably just --
No, there's been weird stuff happening.
I have to go. I'm sorry.

I can't fix your leg now.
I might just make it worse, anyway.
But I'll find out how, and I'll come back really soon, I promise.
Okay.
Hey, Aster? Your magic?
I think it's brilliant.

You're all right!
Mom! What is it?

Do you know where the others are?
What? I was just on a walk.
Tupelo and Aquila. They're missing.
Something is taking our boys.

Something that sneaks through our boundaries and evades us at every turn.
It may be an animal spirit, but what would its motivation be?
It may be a demon we've never encountered before.
We need to stay on our guard.
We need to find out how this monster is getting to us, and where it's keeping our boys.
I refuse to believe they're . . . not alive.
If you kids see anything strange --
anything at all --
let us know.

You all have heard tales, my daughters, of the witches of old, who went into battle against rival clans and evil spirits.
We are lucky to live in this time and this country, where there is peace between witches and the evil spirits are not as bold as they once were.
But I cannot promise you lives free of battle -- especially with the evil that seems to have descended on our family.

And so you must learn about our house's weapons, passed down from mother to daughter since time immemorial.
We have four weapons.
They channel and magnify your will, and can perform various tasks depending on what you desire.
The six stones, for example --
toss them and they will tell you things about the future.

But if you wish to restrain or capture an enemy . . .
A net to trap spirits or the wind or an idea.
Oooooh!

They are vessels for your focus. Now, the dagger hilt --
stones-
future
Excuse me, Iris?
Yes?
Is there one weapon missing?
It looks like there's space for a fifth.
The sword was stolen before you were born, child, by the traitor Mikasi.

He hoped to use it to give himself unnatural powers, but because he was a *man*, it could only have hurt him or else not worked at all.
The dagger, though lesser than the sword, has unique properties . . .
Is that . . . ?
. . . spying again, that's so weird.

Hey, Aster!
Come down!
Hey, Aster, I had a question for you.

Uh, what?
Where even *were* you last night?
When Aquila and 'Pelo went missing?
Because your mom was looking for you for ages.
I was on a walk, I said --
Oh, yeah? Alone or with them?
Because when Sedge was taken, you were *right there*.
Yeah! You were the only one to see him get taken.

What are you saying?
We're just saying you're *weird*.
You don't pay attention in class -- when you even come -- and you're always . . . sneaking around.
I didn't -- I don't *sneak*!
Have you *ever* shifted?
I've never seen it, and you're older than Brome!
heh heh
Leave me alone, Linden.

You're even worse at it than Cygnus!
Hey!
Don't feel bad. You're better than our little friend here.
PAT PAT
Maybe you were jealous that they got their forms?
And you wanted to do something about it?
Don't be stupid, I wasn't jealous of Tupelo and Aquila.
You're *not* jealous that everyone can shift except you?

That mean you finally figured it out?
Come on, Aster, show us.
Turn into something *fierce*.
Like this!
Come on, Aster. Did you do something to Sedge and 'Pelo and Aquila?

Just leave me alone, guys --
What's that?
grrrr
THWAK

Get away --
Leave me alone --
ow! --
Why can't you shift and fight back, Aster?
I think you're a freak. I don't think you *have* any magic.
At least not the right kind.
What is all this?
Give --
it --

-- BACK!
What was that?
He did witchery!

CRK
CRK

chrp
chrp
chrp
chrp
chrp
chrp
chrp
chrp
That was stupid.
chrp

Really, really stupid.
I think I came . . . this way.
Don't want to worry Mom . . .
SNAP!
Stupid, stupid . . .
SNAP
CRK
SNAP

Okay, who's there?
Linden, you'd better not be sneaking up on me --

RRRRRRRR
huuup
RRRRR

Aster?
Aster?
. . . Sedge?
whiiine

SNRRLL

Mom!

Oh, Aster -- my baby --
Mom, that thing . . .
I think it's *Sedge*.

ggRRRR
WHAM
RRRRRRR
This'll have to hold until we can find a way to help him.
Could you pass me the red chalk, dear?

SED
Why're you writing his name?
SEDGF
The containment rune would work for a while, but with the name of its subject, it will be much more powerful.
There's little you can't do if you have the name of a being and the skill.
Oh, they're just --
And what's this bit -- the fiddly drawings around the edge?

Still, Aster?
This magic isn't for you.
I wouldn't even be drawing it with you here if everyone else wasn't in such a tizzy. All these terrible things happening.
SEDGE
Now get --
go back to the house and ask Uncle Kieran if you can help him.
CLK

SLAM
. . . All we know is that something *corrupted* Sedge.
He's still *him*, as far as I can see. The use of his name was efficacious, and . . .
I'll have to look at him with my eyestone in the morning --
But he's been twisted into the worst, most vicious shape he could become.

And we can assume that this is happening to Tupelo and Aquila, as well.
Who knows if Sedge escaped or was set loose?
I've never heard of this happening, never . . .
What do we *do*, then? What do we do for our boy?
Healing magic and time and your love.
If anything can bring him back, it's that.

GRRRRRR
whhiiine

foolish.
foolish to be caught, to hesitate before the kill.
foolish and weak.
SNNRRL
Or did you want to be caught?

Wanted to go back to the witches, wanted them to take care of you?
Wish I could free you, but they've got your name.
Don't hold it against me.

Aunt Iris?
NOK NOK

~HEALING~
~MEDICINE~
~ANATOMY~

Knitting Muscles & Building Bones
Think, Iris . . . kidnappers?
Child thieves?

But not a werewolf -- that certainly couldn't have gotten in . . .
SNAP!
A clever demon, or a powerful one?
Aster! What are you doing here?
Aunt Iris, I wanted to tell you something.

Can it wait, child?
It's about Sedge.
Tell me.
I can't tell my mom.
But the night Sedge vanished . . . I scryed.
And I saw a cave, and there was a voice, and I know I wasn't supposed to --
You most certainly were not!

But it *worked*! I thought you might understand . . .
Bad things happen to boys who dabble with witchery.
Yes, and vice versa, too! I've seen it. Ask Grandmother about her brother, Mikasi, sometime --
I *know*, but can't I help -- ?
No.
SLAM

KNITTING MUSCLE & BUILDING BONE
SNF
SNF

Don't be afraid.
I'm not here to hurt you, little man-child.
A male child of witches and shifters, yes, and one I haven't met yet.
I'm here to make you the same offer I've made to your brothers and cousins, him
They were all so interested, Aquila and Tupelo and Sedge.

Y-you kidnapped them? That was you?
HEL --
ssssshhh
*

You're not in any danger.
If I wanted to hurt you, the witches' boundary wouldn't have let me in.
No, no, no. I simply have... a proposition.
snf
You're different from the others.
You've not found your first form yet, have you?

It's the influence of the witches.
They are jealous of power, and they weaken shifters.
Come with me, though, and I can teach you to shift.
I can show you powerful forms.
Aquila and Tupelo are learning fast.

Sedge? He was weak.
But you... I can smell power on you.

And I'm the only one, little shifter
who can teach you how to use it.

sshhh
Can't risk you speaking of this to the witches, of course.

You won't be able to tell any witch or shifter about this.
They'd only be jealous, you know.
*
Think it over.
And give me a call when you're ready.

Wait!

Juniper, it's almost boiling. Add the dyes.
tap tap
Done!

Mom? Can I --
Not now, Aster!

But I really need to tell you some --
huf huf

Quick, while it's still hot, seal the binding circle.
The circle can't capture anything if we don't know its name, Holly.

I know that, Iris, but it's best to have it prepared.
This circle is powerful enough that as soon as we find out its name, if it even gets close it'll get trapped.
All we need is a name --
Hey! It's Sedge!
He's talking!

What do you remember, sweetness?
It's all hazy, like . . . that time I had the really bad fever.
All twisty.
A cave? Did you find me in a cave?
No, but --
flinch

His voice is finally gone. He was always talking to me, saying . . .
First about giving me the strongest form.
I thought it was part of the ceremony?
And his magic hurt, but it made me strong. He made me . . .
He said bad things about witches, about *all* of you.

And then he said I was too weak -- when I couldn't shift back --
and there was only one thing I could do to be strong . . .
To -- to kill . . .
I'm so sorry . . .
TK
TK
TK
TK
TK
TK
TK

TK TK TK TK TK TK TK
How can you be thinking about it?

This thing is so clearly an evil monster who wants to turn you into a monster, too!
It's more complicated than that.
You're being dumb.
I don't know. It's just . . .
When I think about my life? And the future? What am I going to do?

I can stay with my family, and everyone will think that I just don't have any magic.
That I'm a dud who can't shapeshift.
Maybe if I just never do witchery, it'll go away.
But --
Or I can . . . I don't know, run away? But no magical family would take me in.
And I'd still have to hide my magic from -- from people like you.
Well, that's --
So, I don't know. Is it so crazy to let that thing teach me how to shapeshift?

If I could come home afterward, and if I could finally do the magic everyone wants me to do . . .
I don't think my mom and dad would care that I learned from a monster.
But you said you'd heal my leg.

I don't think I should.
My magic -- it's wrong. I shouldn't use it on other people.
You know how I broke it?
no
There're these boys at school. They're all, like, fifteen, and they have dirt bikes and they're always riding around the woods.
So, they were bothering me, and I kinda . . . made a bet.

I bet that none of them could ride their bikes off this certain cliff and make it to the other side.
And then they said that I had to try, too. And I said if they were scared, I would do it first and show them how it was done, and then . . .
Well, the bike was too big for me to really control it.
How did you --
It wasn't, like, *that* far a drop.

Fifteen feet?
It's good I was wearing a helmet, but I landed on my leg, and . . .
That's . . . terrible. And why . . . ?
I mean, so, you tried to do something you weren't supposed to and you got really hurt?
What are you saying?
The thing is?
I only dared those boys to jump the cliff because I wanted to do it, too.
It was the coolest thing I've ever done, even if I did get hurt. And I'd do it again.

So . . .
Stop feeling sorry for yourself!
Okay.
Okay.
I'm going to heal your leg now.
I'm going to need some things . . .
Knitting Muscle & Building Bone

YELLOW
fsh
Lavender Dream

Oh!
FWOOSH

Can you feel anything?
It feels . . . warm and . . . I dunno -- feels really good actually.
I think it worked!

How long's it going to glow, though?
Oh, uh . . . a while. Until "the magic has run its course."
Says to stay off the leg until then, too.
Aster! What are my dads gonna think?
I don't know, but I have to go.
Can't stay out after sunset anymore.
Aw, they wanted you to stay for dinner. We're making meatloaf!

Sorry.
Um, I hope your leg heals okay!
Can I come over later? If it is?
I have an idea.
Uh . . . yeah, but you can't let anyone see you.
If you go down your street and follow that old dirt road about half a mile, you should be able to see the lights from my house off to the left.
Someone might be patrolling, so be sneaky.
And you're not going to call that evil monster thing, right?

You were right; it was a dumb idea.
You're really good at this magic stuff, Aster.

ssh!

You really shouldn't be here, I'll get in so much trouble if --
Aster! Look at my leg!
I ran all the way here!

Yeah?! It feels okay?
Better than okay.
Why did you bring that?
Come on, now that I know there are *real monsters* out there, I'm not gonna go wandering through the woods to a witch's house without a weapon.
That makes sense.
BOUNCE

Where's the demon phone?
Under the bed.
I think you should call him.
What?
Hear me out!
You can't tell any adults about this, right? And he's gonna keep taking your cousins until you're the only one left.
And who knows if they'll come back and what they'll look like when they do?

But you have a way to get to him, and!
You have the element of surprise! Because you can do *witchery*.
I don't know any spells powerful enough to hurt him.
Weren't you telling me about those weapons? Let's figure out how to get one of them.
Surprise, yeah? I'll stay here, and if something goes wrong, I'll tell your family everything.
There's no magic on *me*.
And then what do I do?
Go rescue your cousins, obviously!

I have no idea what the Beast even is.
have real magic.
Shouldn't you use it for something . . . good?
How to Pick a Lock
CLK

Ooh, take this one!
Okay. And these.

Are you scared?
Uh, yeah. A lot. But . . . you're right. I think I'm the only one who can rescue Tupelo and Aquila.
You might want to hide. I don't know what'll happen.

snf
huff
WHIRRR

So you've decided to come to me, my strange little shifter.

Yeah, I did.
Are my cousins here?
Come inside. What is your name?
Ast -- uh.
What's yours?
...come inside.

23
I've brought another to you, boys.
Our pack grows ever larger.
Strength in numbers, this time, for my assault on the witches.

?
Aster, you're here?
Have you seen my mom? I hope she's not worried.
Tupelo, don't eat that! Can't you see it's rotten?
grrr

Aster, is it?
There is something strange about you, an uneasiness.
I cannot see the Beast inside you, and how can I teach you to change if I don't know what manner of beast you are?
What are you going to do about it?

Where is the part of you that wishes to fight, that longs to kill?
Where is your hate of the witches, of their secrets and lies?
I will need to taste your soul!

The sword was stolen before you were born, child, by the traitor Mikasi.
TSS SSS

Ah!
ugh!

You have the soul of a disgusting
WITCH!
I --
know!
I am a witch, and I know your name, Mikasi!

RRRRRRRR

GRR! SNAP!

Let's go, run!
Get up, come on!
Come on!
GRRR

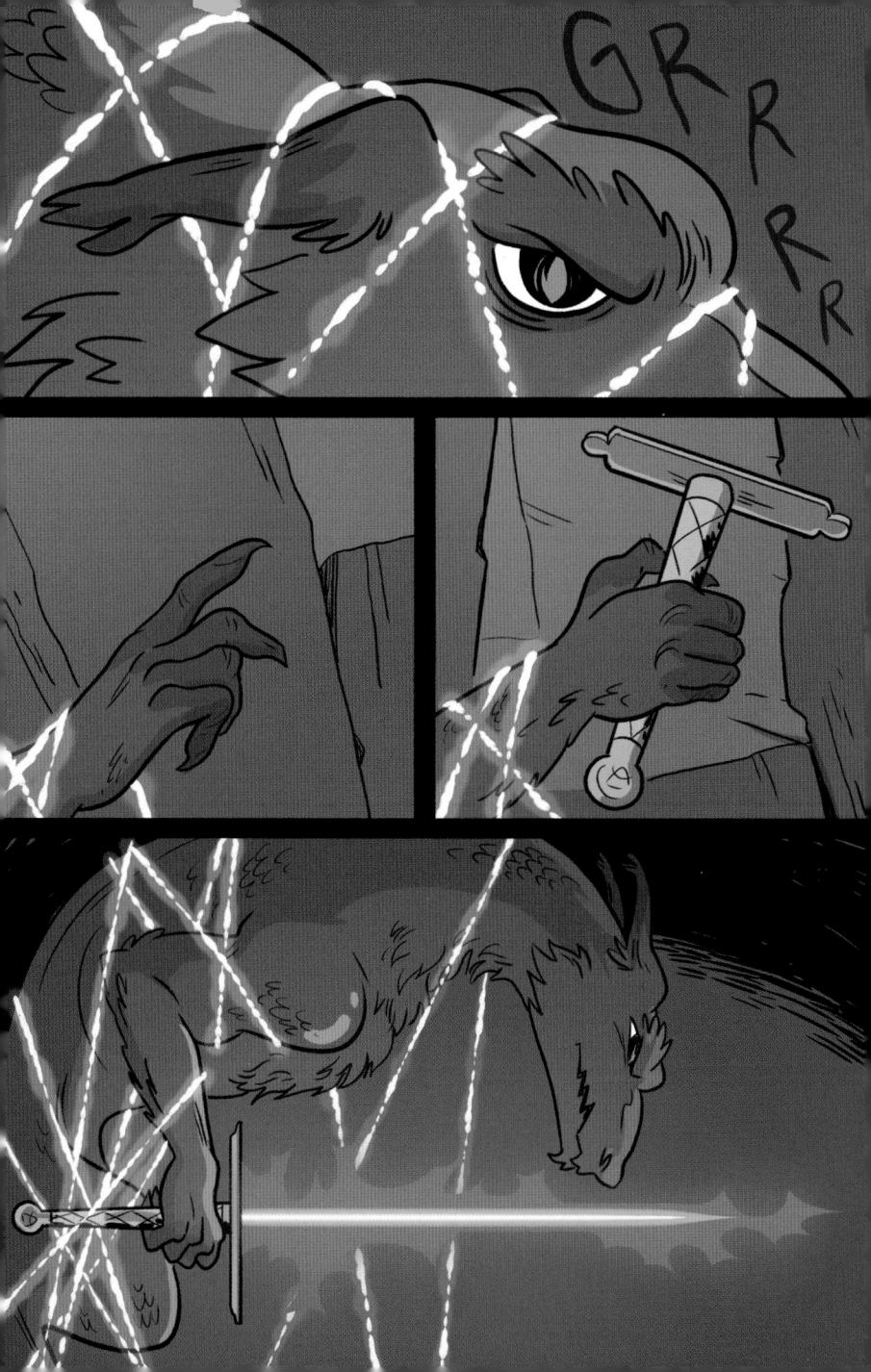
GRRRR

Please work, please work, just take us home --

You did it!

Yeah, but I think he's coming, and I don't know how to close this, and I have to get downstairs --
Go!

SLICE

snf
snf
Now where did they --
CRACK!

GRRRR
CRACK
HSSSSS
GRRAR

WHOOSH
CLATTER
CLATTER
HUF
HUF

Watch out, watch out, he's coming through!

Aster, what's happening?
Stay away from the spell! It's too dangerous --
Mom, you have to trust me!
RUMBLE

CRASH
Get back here, you filthy, little--

No!
ugh
fwoosh

?
SCROWWW

MIKI

LAC

scrch
MIKASI

CLNK

Aster, how . . . ?
Help the boys; they're in Aunt Iris's room. He was poisoning their magic.
And my friend --
I'm okay.
Who is *this*? Aster?
What is this person doing here? What's going on?

Calm yourself, daughter.
Danger has passed.
My brother . . . I never thought I'd see him again in this life.
How did he become like that?

Mikasi never could change his form, not like the other boys.
Used to follow after me, begging for words of power.
Truth to tell, witchery came hard to me, too, in those days.
I was proud of the words I'd learned, yes, and jealous.
Kept them secret, even when my own brother asked me with tears in his eyes to teach him.

Mother, you shouldn't talk about things like this with that . . . girl there.
I've already told her all about magic anyway!
We all kept him from it, told him to learn shifting and be happy with that.
So he tried to use witchery to shapeshift, but it was all wrong.

A black hate grew in him: of me and our mothers and grandmothers, all those who had kept secrets from him.
Even of the other boys. They teased him so much.
He learned a strange kind of shifting that made him turn into monsters, not true animals at all, and hurt him as he shifted.

He left on our eighteenth birthday.
Our family's rejection spurred him to seek someone who would teach him the kind of magic he so desired.
I still had a bond to him -- I could feel his anger and resentment grow as he traveled alone, frustrated in his quest.
I could feel him building a powerful form and becoming trapped in it.
I felt . . .

I felt him try to come home once . . . when he realized what he had become.
We drove him away as a beast and a demon.
I felt the pain drive him mad.
My brother . . .
But surely you did nothing wrong.

Mikasi wanted something that wasn't his . . .
You do not understand, my child, even when the evidence exists in your own son!
Maybe because we shared a womb, but maybe for no reason at all except that witchery was the power he had, the magic he was drawn to.
Mikasi was a witch.
But when we denied him learning, his magic grew, twisted, and hurt him.

Men can't use witchery. Everything forbids it.
Are you so sure?
Or is it because we don't teach men witchery or women shifting?
Mikasi was not the only one who had unexpected magic . . .
. . . but he could not hide it as well as I could.

GASP!
GASP!
I have a little of both -- witchery and shifting -- although I have kept that secret these long years.
But I always knew, just like you, Holly, have never had a moment's doubt that you are a true witch.
And so . . .
Listen to your son when he tells you he is a true witch, too.

I regret what we did to Mikasi every day. It was not his magic that was wrong, but what we denied him.
Don't do the same to Aster.
Aster, I . . . I don't understand.

I've been trying to tell you for a long time.
I love you no matter what, Aster.
We'll figure this out as a family.

. . . Thank you.
I think we have much to learn from each other.

. . . So I'll be starting witchery classes in a few weeks, but Juniper has been showing me some things privately.
She says there's all *kinds* of gaps in what I know!
I've never heard someone be so excited about classes!

Mom and Dad don't really get it, but . . . I don't know, they haven't kicked me out or anything.
So it all worked out!
Yeah, I guess it did.
What about what's his name -- Mikasi?
He's still in the spell.
I think they don't know what to do with him.

Seeing him . . .
He was like me. I could have been like that.
But I won't be.
You? You're way too nice.
Maybe.
If you're studying to be a witch and everything, you'll be really busy, won't you?
You probably won't be able to come over here anymore.

I mean, aren't you not supposed to hang out with . . .
ordinary humans?
Maybe I'm not supposed to. But I think . . .
FLOP
I think maybe I should figure out rules like that for myself.
Like you do.

The reason we're not supposed to be friends is the same reason I'm not supposed to be a witch.
But . . . I am, and we are.
I can't be like my dad or my mom, you know? And I don't want to be like Mikasi . . . ever.
So I just have to be myself.
And I want to be friends with you.
I mean, who wouldn't?

HA
HA
HA

Just stay away from cliffs for a while, okay?
Oh! I wanted to ask: Do you get a flying broom?

A what?
Never mind.
Pass the cookies?

Acknowledgments

I've drawn several graphic novels, but this is the first one I've written, and it's close to my heart.

I'd like to thank my mom, dad, and everyone else in our family for being so supportive of my unusual interests and implausible goals. I feel your love every day and I hope you feel mine, too.

I'd like to thank my friends — the people I know from summer camp, art school, comic conventions, animation, and the Internet. Your talent pushes me to work harder, and your kindness makes me a better person.

I'd like to thank my agent, Jen Linnan, who is fiercely smart, warm, and has been with me for every step on this journey.

I'd also like to thank my editor, Amanda Maciel, and my art director, Phil Falco, whose expertise and advice were a huge help in bringing this book into the world.

I drew this book during a year of many changes, and my partner was with me through them all. She believed in me even when I didn't. Thank you, Noelle — I love you and the home we've made together so very much.

DEVELOPMENT
ART

Aster, along with all the other kids in the family, mostly wears hand-me-downs, and accessorizes with protection charms made for him by his mother. His favorite color is purple and he doesn't like getting haircuts.

Even when Charlie has her leg in a cast, she still dresses like she's ready to play basketball or baseball at the drop of a hat. In an earlier draft of this story, she didn't have a broken leg, which is why there's a design of her without a cast.

This is early concept art of Aster, when I thought he'd be older. I always knew, though, that he liked to find out-of-the-way places to read through his spell book.

Holly is a perfect witch. She's powerful, practical, beautiful, and kind, and I wanted her character design to reflect that.

Like Holly, Tohor is a perfect example of a shapeshifter. He always knows what to do, he loves his family, and he's in touch with nature.

I had a lot of different designs for Mikasi, but I decided in the end to make him into a kind of dragon monster. He used magic to force himself to transform so many times that he became a mishmash of different animals—a coyote's face, a crocodile's body, and a human's hands.

MOLLY KNOX OSTERTAG grew up in the forests of upstate New York, where she spen the first half of her childhood reading about fantastica adventures and the second half acting them out with foam swords at a live-action role-playing group. She graduated in 2014 from the School of Visual Arts, where she studied cartooning and illustration; she now lives in Los Angeles California. *The Witch Boy* is her middle-grade graphic nove debut. You can visit Molly online at www.mollyostertag.com